A Pug Called Poppy

A Pug Called Poppy

Paul Nicholas Mason

Illustrated by

Sara Berrino

$|$ N$_1$ $|$ O$_2$ $|$ N$_1$

CANADA

*Publisher's note: This book is a work of fiction. Names, characters, places and
incidents are either the product of the author's imagination or are used
fictitiously, and any resemblance to actual persons living or dead
is entirely coincidental.*

Library and Archives Canada Cataloguing in Publication

Mason, Paul Nicholas
[Short Stories. Selections]
A pug called Poppy / Paul Nicholas Mason.

Short stories.
ISBN 978-1-988098-35-7 (softcover)

I. Title.

PS8576.A85955A6 2017   jC813'.54   C2017-904644-6

Printed and bound in Canada on 100% recycled paper.

Now Or Never Publishing
#313, 1255 Seymour Street
Vancouver, British Columbia
Canada V6B 0H1

nonpublishing.com
Fighting Words.

We gratefully acknowledge the support of the Canada Council for the Arts
and the British Columbia Arts Council for our publishing program.

To Denise Adele Heaps, Mother of Pugs

and

To Rachael, Fernando and Baby-Gillian

Contents

Chapter One

POPPY MEETS SMUDGE

THE FIRST TIME Poppy the Pug met Smudge the Maine Coon Cat, she didn't like him much. To be fair, Smudge didn't like her either. Now of course, cats and dogs are naturally suspicious of each other, so it's no surprise they didn't *instantly* become friends.

Poppy lived with her human, Danielle, a high school teacher, in a nice little house in a friendly neighbourhood in Peterborough, Ontario. The house had a smallish living room, and a biggish kitchen, and a laundry nook and two bedrooms and one large bathroom. Danielle didn't live with another human, so she and Poppy had it all to themselves, and Poppy had her very own little bed next to Danielle's big bed.

Danielle was fond of bold colours – rich purples and emerald greens and dazzling reds. (Poppy herself was a glossy black pug.) Their home was filled with pillows and cushions and paintings of places Danielle had visited all over the world. And Danielle had books – lots and lots and lots of books. Poppy didn't really understand the point of books, but she saw they made her human happy. Danielle liked to read her books with Poppy sleeping beside her, and Poppy liked that, too. The house smelled like roses, which was the base note in Danielle's perfume.

Smudge the cat lived with *his* human, Pam. Pam had a house in the same neighbourhood, and she worked in a store. From the outside, her house looked a little like Danielle's, but inside the walls were painted taupe — which is a sort of greyish brown. Taupe was a very popular colour with interior designers, and Pam had a talent for making her house look like the sort of house you'd see in a magazine.

Poppy and Smudge met at the dog park near Danielle's home. Danielle had brought Poppy to the park, and was letting her run around and get some exercise. Smudge had come over to the dog park — which he thought should really be a *cat* park — on his own. It was on his cat-trail route, which took him all around the neighbourhood every day that Pam let him out.

"Where's your human?" asked Poppy the first time she met Smudge. "Animals are only allowed in this park if they come with their human."

"That rule only applies to dogs," said Smudge a little haughtily. "Cats can go wherever they like, whenever they like. We're special."

"Dogs are special, too," said Poppy indignantly. "But we know there are rules you have to obey."

"There aren't any rules for cats," said Smudge. Smudge knew that wasn't absolutely true, because, for instance, he was expected to use the cat box when he wanted to go to the bathroom at home, and Pam wouldn't let him get up on the kitchen counters or the dining room table. Still, he felt that Poppy was challenging his right to be in the park, and he didn't like that.

"Poppy!" called Danielle. "Leave the big cat alone, sweetie, and get some exercise."

So Poppy trotted off, and then raced around a little just for the joy of feeling the wind in her face, but she kept an eye on Smudge – and so it was that she saw Psycho-Cat approaching him from behind.

Psycho-Cat was the most unfriendly animal in the Thompson Bay neighbourhood. No, that's not quite right. He wasn't simply unfriendly; he was *hostile*. Some humans are bullies, and some animals are, too. If Psycho-Cat had been human, the police would have arrested him and hauled him off to jail. But because he was an animal and didn't hurt humans (unless they tried to pet his head or rub his tummy), the police left Psycho-Cat alone and he was free to kill birds and field mice and beat up other cats. Even small dogs like Poppy were scared of Psycho-Cat, and on one occasion several months before, Poppy had seen a big German Shepherd turn and slink away rather than cross Psycho-Cat.

Smudge, for his part, was big, but he was gentle. He liked people. He wanted to be friends with other cats. And his human, Pam, had had him de-clawed, so even if he'd wanted to fight – and he didn't – he would not have been very successful.

Poppy guessed that any encounter between Smudge and Psycho-Cat was going to end very badly for Smudge. "Look out!" she barked at Smudge: "Psycho-Cat is sneaking up behind you!"

Smudge turned, but it was too late for him to run away. Psycho-Cat was now very near him – just a pounce away. After a moment's thought, Smudge lay down on his side, his paws on the ground, to signal that he didn't want to fight.

Psycho-Cat sneered. "What sort of 'fraidy-Cat just gives up? Are you too scared to defend yourself?"

"I don't like to fight," Smudge said. "My human says I'm a lover, not a fighter."

"Well, I'm bored," hissed Psycho-Cat. "I need some exercise. So you get up on your lazy paws and defend yourself – or run off home to your silly human!" And with that he leapt forward and began to swipe and claw at Smudge's face and body. Smudge howled in fear and tried desperately to fend Psycho-Cat off, but he didn't stand a chance.

Now, Poppy wasn't a friend of Smudge's, and she was just a small black pug, but she didn't like to see another creature hurt. She hesitated for only a fraction of a second before launching herself toward the fighting felines, barking wildly. "Poppy!" shouted Danielle – but Poppy kept going and barrelled straight into Psycho-Cat, knocking him off Smudge and sending him sprawling.

Psycho-Cat was up on his paws almost immediately. But while he would willingly have taken on both Poppy and Smudge at the same time, he didn't want to tangle with an angry human – and Danielle was advancing on him now waving her arms and shouting, "Bad cat! Shoo! Go on!" He stood still a moment, looked meaningfully at Poppy and Smudge, then hissed, "See you later, *pets*," and slunk away.

Danielle scooped Poppy up in her arms. "Oh, Poppy, you're such a brave little dog," she said. "And that was so nice of you to help out this kitty. I didn't know you were friends!"

Poppy allowed herself to be adored for a moment or two before she squirmed to get down. She didn't mind cuddling with Danielle when it was just the two of them alone at home, but she was a little embarrassed by public displays of affection.

Smudge had not moved. "Thank you," he said quietly. "That was nice of you. I didn't see him coming."

"Oh, that's okay," said Poppy. "I could see you needed a little help." And then, kindly: "We all need a little help now and then."

"That's true," said Smudge, and he nodded thoughtfully. "Well," he added, "I'll see you again soon," and he turned tail and headed off in the opposite direction of Psycho-Cat.

Poppy stood watching him go. She felt a little bit proud of herself – a feeling of which pugs are very fond – and she also sensed that she had made a friend.

"Let's go home now, Poppy," said Danielle. "We've had enough excitement for today, and I expect you'd like your dinner and I'd like a bath." So the two of them headed off home together, the human and her glossy black pug, a quiet, companionable night ahead of them.

Chapter Two

A NEW MAN-FRIEND
FOR DANIELLE

THE DAY AFTER Poppy met Smudge for the first time – and bravely fought off Psycho-Cat – she met someone else who was to become important in her life.

It was a Saturday, so Danielle didn't have to teach. Saturdays were Poppy's favourite day – along with Sundays and the other days of the week. (Like most dogs, Poppy found many things pretty special in the moment they happened.) Saturdays were special because Danielle often stayed home all day, and because the two of them, the dog and her human, sometimes took two *long* walks together.

On this Saturday, the day unfolded pretty much like every other Saturday. Danielle slept in a little, then took Poppy for a *little* walk (to do what every dog needs to do after a long night), then gave Poppy breakfast, then had a leisurely breakfast herself. And on this Saturday Poppy got the scraps of Danielle's breakfast, as a treat for being a glossy black pug. Then Danielle did some house-cleaning, which Poppy enjoyed helping with – apart from the vacuuming, which was much too noisy and completely unnecessary. There was a part of Poppy that found the whole idea of vacuuming a bit insulting. Danielle seemed to give extra attention to the areas where Poppy slept and played, sucking up the fur that Poppy quite deliberately shed in these places.

After the house-cleaning was over, Danielle did some laundry, and Poppy helped with that by jumping into the laundry baskets and burrowing under the clothes. On this Saturday, too, Poppy made herself useful by knocking over a box of detergent and spilling some of its contents on the floor. Danielle wasn't as grateful for that as Poppy had hoped she might be, but she soon recovered her good humour and made a cup of tea and settled down to read a book. Meanwhile, Poppy napped beside her to recover from all the hard work she had done.

After lunch Danielle cleaned up the kitchen and mopped the floor and then took Poppy for the first of what Poppy hoped would be two long walks. They trotted along the Rotary Greenway trail that had once been a railway track, and Poppy smelled all sorts of delicious smells. She barked at a squirrel, and barked at a bird, and ate some grass, and barked at a chipmunk, and generally reminded the universe that she was keeping watch over things in the way that only a little black pug can. It was a great walk – quite possibly the best walk that Poppy had had since the day before when, as you scarcely need reminding, she had met Smudge and showed Psycho-Cat she was a force to be reckoned with.

When they got home, however, the tempo of the day seemed to change. Danielle became a little agitated. She remembered to give Poppy some fresh water in her bowl and a little doggy biscuit, but she didn't seem as patient as she usually was when Poppy barked at people passing by on the street. And she spent a long time talking on the telephone – much, much longer than was necessary.

As the day wore on, Poppy became more and more aware that her human was distracted. And things became worse when, a little later in the afternoon, Danielle began cooking something that required a great deal of her attention. Yes, there was another walk, but it was just a *little* walk, and once it was over Danielle ran herself a bath, and ironed a pretty black dress. She told Poppy sternly that she was not to get up on the bed.

Now often when Danielle had a bath she took a big glass of red wine in with her and a book by one of her favourite feminist authors. She would lie in the bath and drink her wine and read her book and say things like, "Right on, sister!" or "You go, girl!" On this occasion, however, she seemed much more focused than usual: she washed her hair and shaved her legs and after she got out of the bath she went to check on her cooking. Poppy did her best to distract her by dragging her bowl into the middle of the kitchen, but Danielle simply patted her head and told her to be a good dog. "I *am* a good dog," Poppy thought indignantly.

And then, half an hour later, and after Danielle had put on her nicely-ironed dress, there came a knock at the door. A moment later, a man with a bald head and a deep voice was standing inside the entry hall, smelling of leather and spice. He was carrying a bottle of wine and a bunch of flowers – both gifts apparently intended for Danielle, though Poppy would have enjoyed eating the flowers – and he kissed

Danielle in a way that Poppy found far too familiar. "Poppy, this is Andrew," said Danielle.

"Oh, what a nice Doberman," said Andrew, bending down to pet Poppy. Poppy snorted. Anyone capable of making such a silly mistake would surely be ordered to leave the house immediately, but Danielle just laughed and said "Andrew!" and then kissed him again. And when that happened, Poppy suddenly realized, with a sinking of her puggy heart, that this Andrew character might be around for a little while.

And things got still worse as the evening went on. After Danielle and Andrew had eaten dinner, and after Andrew had done the dishes (which Danielle made a huge fuss over), the two humans went into the living room and put on a movie. When Poppy took her usual place beside her human companion, Andrew gently but unceremoniously lifted her up and put her on Danielle's other side, taking Poppy's side all to himself.

★★★

The very next day, Poppy happened to see Smudge again when Poppy was on one of her walks around the neighbourhood with Danielle. Danielle had paused to talk with Mrs. Cairns, a nice old lady who lived up the street, and Smudge crossed the street to say "hello."

"How are you?" asked Poppy.

"I'm fine, thank you, said Smudge. "Just a couple of bruises and one cut – but my human put something on the cut."

"Did it hurt?" asked Poppy sympathetically. "Yes," said Smudge, "but she said she had to do it to make sure I didn't get a fection."

"A *fection*?" repeated Poppy. "Isn't that like a cuddle?"

"I don't think so," said Smudge. "I think it's what happens when something goes wrong in a cut."

The two animals thought about that for a moment. It was a puzzling thing. (And, indeed, whether you're a glossy black pug or a large and friendly Maine Coon cat, the whole idea of *in*fections is very difficult to grasp.)

"Is anything going on in your life?" asked Smudge.

"Well, now that you ask," said Poppy, "Danielle had a man-friend over to the house last night for dinner. And he stayed a long time."

"Was he nice?" asked Smudge. "Sometimes man-friends can be nice."

"No," said Poppy. "He called me a Doberman, and he lifted me out of my rightful place when we were watching a movie."

"Did he put you outside?" asked Smudge.

"Certainly not!" said Poppy – scandalized at the thought that anyone might even *think* of doing that.

"Did he put you on the floor?" asked Smudge.

"Well, no," said Poppy. "He put me on the other side of Danielle."

"Hmm," said Smudge. "That doesn't sound too horrible. I think I'd give him a chance. My human has man-friends. Some of them like cats."

"I'll think about it," said Poppy. And, as Danielle's chat with Mrs. Cairns was wrapping up she added, "See you later!"

"See you later," said Smudge — and he trotted off down the road, eager for new adventures but keeping his eyes wide open for signs of Psycho-Cat.

★★★

So Poppy did give Andrew a chance. A few days later, when he showed up on the doorstep yet again, and was greeted by a very friendly kiss from Danielle, Poppy didn't growl or bark. Well, not much. Instead, she gave him an opportunity to pat and ruffle her head, and trotted after him when he went into the living room with her human. And her forbearance was rewarded when, a few moments later, Andrew suddenly broke off from his conversation with Danielle and exclaimed, "Oh! I brought a little something for your pug!"

"Is it a toy?" asked Danielle. "Poppy really likes toys."

"No," said Andrew, "I'm afraid I didn't think of that. It's food." And he got up and went out to his coat in the hallway and took a small container of something from its pocket. "I noticed that she was eating dry food," he said, "and I thought she might enjoy something, um, *meatier*. If you don't mind, of course."

Now if there is one thing pugs like more than toys, it's food. Pugs are always thinking about food: what it tastes like, when they might get it, how they might get *more* of it, how they might get it faster, and how they can keep anyone else from stealing it from their bowls. When Poppy saw that Andrew had brought her a gift of food her little eyes grew larger and rounder than they usually were.

"You've made a friend for life!" said Danielle, laughing. She led Andrew into the kitchen where he scooped up Poppy's food bowl and washed it. This was completely unnecessary in Poppy's eyes, as the lingering smells of the last meal were to her mind a splendid thing. Then he opened the plastic container, spooned the contents out into the bowl, and put the bowl back on to the floor. Poppy turned three complete circles while Andrew was on his way to the bowl rack, then thrust her muzzle into the dinner he'd brought for her.

And if bringing food wasn't enough – and it was an impressive thing all by itself – later that day, while Danielle was doing the dishes and washing her hair, Andrew took Poppy for a brisk long walk around the neighbourhood. They even ventured into the Trent University Wildlife Sanctuary, a place so full of exotic smells and sounds that the little pug could barely contain her excitement. She decided, upon their return to her home, that while Andrew seemed poised to take a lot of Danielle's time and energy, he also had some qualities that a pug could feel pretty good about. When he eventually settled on the couch to have a cup of tea and talk to a clean-haired Danielle, Poppy jumped up beside him, settled her chin on his leg, and was soon snoring musically.

Chapter Three

SMUDGE GETS A NEW NAME

NOW, AS WE'VE already learned, Smudge's human companion, Pam – who had painted all her walls taupe – would often let Smudge out of the house when she went to work. Smudge would go off on what Pam called his cat-trail, wandering all over the neighbourhood and exploring anything that caught his interest. This worked pretty well during the spring, summer and fall (unless it was windy), but Smudge found the winters a little harsh. He sometimes wished that Pam would set up a cat-door that would allow him to come inside when his paws were cold.

One day shortly after Andrew came into Poppy's life, Smudge set off on the cat-trail. Finding the day windier than he'd expected, he was happy to take refuge in an open garage where someone had thoughtfully left a pile of newspapers in the corner. Smudge liked the smell of newspapers, so he made himself comfortable, and because it had been a particularly active morning and afternoon, he fell asleep. He woke up just as the garage door was closing, the owners of the house having apparently used a remote to do so. He wasn't terribly worried at first, however, and simply went back to sleep. Smudge liked to sleep.

But when night came, and the hour at which Pam would have returned from work passed, Smudge woke up and began thinking about his dinner (and about Pam, too, of whom Smudge was very fond in spite of her weakness for taupe).

And by the time midnight rolled around, and the garage door had still not opened, Smudge was a hungry and sad Maine Coon cat.

Cats can express sadness in all sorts of ways, but on this particular evening Smudge chose to *vocalize* his feelings. He sat up very straight, leaned his head back, and began to sing a little song about how hungry and sad he was. He put his heart into it. "A-waa-waa-waa-waa!" he sang. "A-waa-waa-waa-waa-waa!"

Some animals sing very sweetly. Many members of the bird kingdom, for example, trill and peep in ways that warm the human heart. Little puppies just finding their voices can sound very cute. The writer of these stories is very fond of the snuffly noises that otters make to one another. But the fully-grown Maine Coon cat does not have a musical voice. The fully-grown Maine Coon cat has a voice that can shatter glass and curl human hair.

Poppy the Pug was fast asleep in her little bed beside Danielle's big bed when Smudge began to sing. She woke with a start, thinking at first that she must have had a very bad dream. (Danielle was a bit hard of hearing, so she slept on.) It took a moment for Poppy to realize that the noise was the song of her friend Smudge. But when she did she jumped up on the bed and tried to wake her human companion.

"Go back to sleep, Mr. Darcy," said Danielle, from the depths of a very pleasant dream. It was clear that she did not want to be woken.

Poppy cocked her head and listened very carefully to Smudge's sad song. The details were not very clear, but she quickly understood that he was hungry and lonely and locked in somewhere he definitely didn't want to be. What was a glossy black pug to do? Poppy pondered the question very seriously. And then she realized she might have a solution. Andrew was spending the night – though he was, of course, sleeping in the *spare* bedroom – so Poppy jumped off the bed, nosed open Danielle's bedroom door, and raced down the hall. Then she head-butted Andrew's door, and jumped up onto his bed barking.

Andrew sat bolt upright in bed. (He was not at all hard of hearing!) "Shakira!" he gasped, clearly in the grip of his own dream. "What? Oh, it's you, Poppy."

Poppy was a gifted glossy black pug, but she could not speak human language. She tried to convey the nature of the problem by encouraging Andrew to listen. To do that, she cocked her head and listened herself.

"Oh!" said Andrew again, after a moment. "What's that horrible noise, Poppy?"

Recognizing that she'd been successful, Poppy jumped down from the bed, pulling the sheet and coverlet with her, and made for the door. She turned and looked back reproachfully at Andrew when he did not immediately follow her.

"Do you want me to follow you?" asked Andrew, a little slow on the uptake.

"Of course I do!" barked Poppy. "Come on, human!"

"Just a moment," said Andrew. "I'll have to put on some pants first."

Four minutes later Poppy and Andrew arrived at the house down the street (and around the corner) from whose garage Smudge's sad song was emanating. Poppy had led the way, of course, but Andrew, now that he was thoroughly awake, had followed at a decent trot. They went up the driveway together and Poppy gave a quick bark at the garage. "It's me, Smudge!" she said. "I'm here! And I brought Danielle's boy!"

Smudge stopped singing. "Is that you, Poppy?" he called. "I'm locked in. I can't get out!"

Poppy looked meaningfully at Andrew. "Do something," she yipped.

Andrew rubbed his head and stared at the garage door. "I don't know, Poppy," he said. "I feel a bit strange opening someone else's garage door. And I really don't want to bang on the *front* door at this time of night either."

It seemed obvious to Poppy that if anybody was home, they must be much deafer than Danielle – but that was too complicated an idea to express with just a look and a bark. She contented herself with staring at Andrew, waiting for him to come to his senses and take action.

"Well, all right," said Andrew with a sigh. "I don't suppose it would do any harm to open the garage door just a few inches." He put his hand on the handle, and, with a little effort, raised it about a foot. Smudge shot out of the garage, almost tripping over himself in his relief at being freed.

"Thank you!" he said. "That was awful! I'm hungry!"

Andrew pushed the garage door down, then turned to look at the two animals. "What on earth were you doing in there, Big Cat?" he said. "This isn't your home, is it? Danielle told me that a Maine Coon lives a couple of streets away."

"That's right," said Smudge, though he, like Poppy, knew that Andrew would not really understand him. It was all very frustrating, but he felt grateful to Andrew for rescuing him, and to Poppy for bringing the human to the garage door. He rubbed up against Andrew's legs to show his appreciation.

"Okay," said Andrew, "let's get you home, Kitty, then Poppy and I can go back to our beds." And so the human, the Maine Coon cat, and the glossy black pug trotted off down the road together until they reached Pam's house, where Andrew knocked on the door.

Just a moment passed, and a voice could be heard from inside the house. "Who is it?" said Pam's voice. She sounded very worried.

"My name is Andrew," said Andrew. "I think I may have your cat."

Pam swiftly unlocked the door and looked out. "Smudge!" she said. "Oh, you bad cat! Where have you been?" And then, turning to Andrew: "Thank you so much for finding him. I've been worried sick."

"You have Poppy the Pug to thank," said Andrew. "And it was our pleasure to bring *Mr.* Smudge back home safe and sound." And he and Poppy turned and went back down Pam's driveway and headed for home. Not for the first time, and surely not for the last, Poppy felt a warm flush of pride at her swift and effective action. And she also felt, and she sensed that Andrew might agree, that she deserved a treat (or two) as a reward.

Smudge, meanwhile, was tucking into a very late dinner, and reflecting on the fact that he rather liked being called *Mr.* Smudge. It was a good, *masculine* name. And when a cat has been declawed and neutered and lives in a house with taupe walls, a little respect goes a long way.

Chapter Four

A VISIT TO
WENDA'S WHITE HOUSE

JUST THREE STREETS away from the home of
Danielle and Poppy the Pug there lived a very
nice young couple called Rachael and
Fernando and their lovely nine-month old
baby, Gillian. Danielle and Poppy often ran
into Rachael and Gillian at the neighbourhood

park – which was a different park altogether from the dog park.

Danielle and Rachael would sometimes sit on a bench and chat with each other. Rachael would hold little Gillian, and Poppy would sit beside Danielle, and they would all watch the older children playing on the slide and swings and jungle gym. In this way Poppy came to know Rachael and Gillian – at least well enough that she would sneeze on Rachael's leg (which is one of the rather strange ways that pugs show affection). Rachael, for her part, would always greet Poppy with a pat on the head, and Gillian would make a very excited sound whenever she saw the glossy black pug.

Rachael belonged to a mothers-and-children-coffee-and-play-group that met every Thursday morning in the home of one of the moms and kids – a different home each week. On this particular Thursday Danielle had a nasty cold and had stayed home from school: she was marking essays in the spare bedroom when Poppy came to tell her that she would like to go for a walk.

"Poppy, I can't take you for a walk right now," said Danielle. "I took you for a walk an hour ago and I feel awful and I have six essays to mark before I can get up from my chair."

Poppy felt sorry for Danielle, but she had looked out the living-room window just a moment before and seen her friend Mr. Smudge the Maine Coon cat skulking around on the road and glancing hopefully at her home, and she felt it might be nice to have a little chat. She stood her ground, then, and looked at Danielle reproachfully with her round, sad eyes.

"Okay," said Danielle. "If I let you out for a few minutes, will you promise me to stay in the front yard? I don't want you running on to the road and getting hit by a car or going down the street and pooping on one of our neighbours' lawns."

Poppy felt very indignant at this because she prided herself on never pooping on a lawn if there was a strip of public land available – and she only relieved herself at all, of course, when Danielle was right there with a little bag. She barked crossly.

"Okay, then," said Danielle, getting up to let Poppy out. "But don't you forget that you've made me a promise."

Once outside, Poppy waited for Danielle to go back in the house, then gave a short little yip to let Mr. Smudge know she was there. He quickly appeared from behind the community mailboxes across the street, where he had been hanging out casually. (Cats are good at hanging out casually.)

"Hello, Poppy," said Mr. Smudge.

"Hello, Mr. Smudge," said Poppy. She had quickly learned that her feline friend was very fond of his new title.

"I'm glad you could come out for a chat," said Mr. Smudge.

"Oh, I can come out any time I like," said Poppy. (Now, of course, this wasn't quite true, but small dogs do sometimes need to brag a little.)

"How is your human?" asked Mr. Smudge politely.

"She's got a cold," said Poppy, "and it's making her unreasonable. I'm a bit cross with her right now."

"Why?" asked Mr. Smudge.

"Well," said Poppy, "she told me I had to stay in the front yard. And that doesn't seem very fair."

"Perhaps she's worried you might be hit by a car," said the Mr. Smudge. "Some humans aren't very careful when they drive."

"I know to be careful," said Poppy. "I always look both ways before I cross the road."

"I'm sure you do," said Mr. Smudge soothingly.

At just that instant both Poppy and Mr. Smudge saw Rachael coming round the corner just a few houses down the street. She had baby Gillian in a Snugli, and a diaper bag in her left hand.

"That's Rachael and Gillian," said Poppy.

"It's Thursday," said Mr. Smudge. "They're probably going to that play-date thing most of the mothers and babies go to on Thursdays."

"Does your human go?" asked Poppy.

"No," said Mr. Smudge. "She doesn't have a baby. I think sometimes she wishes she did."

As the animals watched, Rachael began going up one of the driveways toward the front door of a home with an immaculate front yard. The grass looked like the grass on a golf-course, and the shrubs and trees were pruned into perfect circles and cones.

"I like babies," said Poppy. "They smell interesting, and they're always dropping food."

"I like babies, too," said Mr. Smudge. "And mommies."

"You know what?" said Poppy. "I bet they're eating cookies at this moms-and-babies thing. And I bet that some of the nice moms would want to give us cookies and pat us on the head."

"I've never eaten a cookie," said Mr. Smudge. "Are they tasty?"

"Cookies are the best things ever," said Poppy the Pug. "I could eat cookies all day long and never get full. I could eat twenty-hundred cookies in two minutes and then eat twenty-hundred more and not even feel a little bit sick."

"Hmm," said Mr. Smudge.

"So let's go!" said Poppy.

"Where?" said Mr. Smudge. "To the moms-and-babies thing? But we don't have our humans with us. And we don't have babies."

"We're *fur*-babies, aren't we?" said Poppy. "That's what Danielle calls me."

"But didn't your human tell you that you have to stay in your front yard?" said Mr. Smudge. He didn't want his friend to get in trouble.

"We won't be gone long," said Poppy, "and Danielle likes it when I'm friendly. She would probably *want* me to go if she knew it was happening. She would probably say, 'Poppy, you scamper on down the street and be social with those nice moms and their babies.'" Now, Poppy didn't really know that her human would say anything of the kind, but when she said the words out loud it certainly seemed the sort of thing that Danielle *ought* to say.

"Well, all right," said Mr. Smudge. The two friends looked around for a moment to see if they were being watched, and, confident that they weren't, trotted down the street toward the house with the front lawn like a golf course.

When once they arrived, they looked around again, then went straight up to the front door.

"How are we going to get in?" said Mr. Smudge. He was a clever cat, and he had learned that bedroom and bathroom doors could sometimes be pushed open if Pam hadn't closed them all the way, but front doors were a different thing altogether. People usually closed front doors firmly.

"There's always a way," said Poppy the Pug. "Just let me think for a moment." She sat down on her haunches and thought, and to make sure she was using time efficiently she gave herself a good scratch, too, her back paw finding just the right spot behind her right ear.

"Do you have fleas?" asked Mr. Smudge sympathetically.

"Certainly not!" said Poppy, much affronted by the idea. And at that moment, the front door suddenly opened and a woman neither animal recognized came out.

"I'm just getting Emma's pacifier from the car," said the strange woman, calling back into the house – but before she could close the door, Poppy the Pug slipped around her and into the warmth of the hallway, leaving her friend Mr. Smudge on the front step. "Aren't you a big cat!" said the strange woman to Mr. Smudge. "And was that Wenda's doggie I just let into the house?"

"Well, no," said Mr. Smudge, who was as honest as he was big – but of course the woman didn't understand him, and she was focused on getting her baby's pacifier anyway. So he waited patiently until she returned from her car, and then slipped into the house on her heels when she went back in.

Poppy, meanwhile, had been checking out the lay of the land. She was confident that most of the moms would be glad to see her – who, after all, can resist a pug? she reasoned – but something told her she should choose her moment wisely. So to avoid making a premature entrance she went about halfway up the stairs, which led off the front hall, and lay down on a step to sniff the air and think about things. She hoped, too, that her friend Mr. Smudge would join her in the house when

once the unfamiliar lady returned from her car —
which is exactly what happened.

"I'm up here, Mr. Smudge," she yipped
when he came in, and he quickly bounded up
the stairs towards her, giving the mother of
Emma the strong impression that he too
belonged in the house. She went back into the
living room brandishing the pacifier and cooing
at the baby she had left in another mother's arms.

"What do we do now?" asked Mr. Smudge.
He wasn't feeling quite the same confidence
Poppy was that he'd be well received. He *hoped*
she was right, but he'd had enough experience in
the world to know that not everyone is happy to
see a Maine Coon cat. On one memorable
occasion he'd been mistaken for a skunk, and
that confusion had made him cautious.

"We should make our appearance when we
hear plates and spoons and eating noises," said
Poppy. "That's when humans are in their best
moods. And when we hear those things we
should go right in and look as cute as we know
how — and then they'll give us cookies."

Mr. Smudge thought about this for a moment. "Might they give us fish?" he asked hopefully.

"I don't think so," said Poppy. "At least, I don't smell any fish. Do you?"

Both animals breathed in deeply. The house was full of interesting odours, but neither could smell fish. Mr. Smudge felt a little bit sad, but he could smell cheese, and milk, and he figured that he might get a mouthful or two of something interesting, as well as some nice pats and ruffles. Mr. Smudge liked pats and ruffles. Public displays of affection were just fine with him.

So the two friends waited on the stairs, and in truth they didn't have long to wait before it became clear to them that the hostess had picked up trays from the kitchen and had taken them into the living room, and that all the moms were now loading up their plates with little snacks and nibblies.

"Are you ready?" asked Poppy the Pug.

"Yes," said Mr. Smudge, hesitating for only a fraction of a second – and then he followed his friend down the stairs, through the hallway, and into the large, tastefully-decorated living room of the woman called Wenda.

We should probably pause here to say a few words about Wenda and her family. Wenda's husband was a very nice, gentle sort of man, and he had learned, over the course of his marriage, that it was a good idea to do as his wife asked him. Wenda liked her front lawn to look like a golf course, so Wenda's husband spent a lot of time and money making it look like one. Wenda liked her shrubs pruned into geometric shapes, so her husband bought a pair of electric garden clippers, watched a video or two on YouTube, and learned how to produce the shapes his wife desired. Wenda liked her house white, so her husband painted all the walls a clean eggshell colour, and bought white sofas and white armchairs and white shag rugs. Everything in Wenda's house was very clean – and, to be fair, Wenda was very good at cleaning.

Now, when Poppy the Pug and Mr. Smudge the Maine Coon cat made their appearance, many another mom might have laughed and said "hello," and maybe even given them a treat or two before showing them to the door . . . but Wenda was not that kind of mom. "Aaarrrggghhh! – stray animals! Fleas! Rabies!" she shouted, and she charged at Poppy and Smudge waving her arms and stamping her feet.

Mr. Smudge was startled by this, of course, and he immediately shrank his body as close to the floor as he possibly could and tried to blend into the rug . . . but Poppy was shocked! And when a pug is shocked she sometimes has a most unfortunate biological response – and so it was that while Poppy had certainly refrained from pooping on Wenda's lawn, she now left her mark, so to speak, on Wenda's white shag rug.

We will draw a curtain over the next few moments because they were filled with noise and upset and disturbance. Wenda yelled, and babies cried, and Mr. Smudge howled and Poppy barked and the mothers talked very loudly and Wenda yelled some more. It was not the most successful meeting of the moms-and-babies club, and it ended with Rachael and Baby-Gillian delivering a rather subdued Poppy to Danielle's house, with news that did not make Danielle feel any better (though Rachael tried hard to describe things in a funny way).

So that is the story of how the bad feelings between Wenda and Poppy the Pug began, and of how Danielle came briefly to feel reluctant to let Poppy out of the house at all on her own, and of how Mr. Smudge learned that, brave and wonderful though his pug-friend was, it remained a good idea to think for himself and not always follow her lead. When, some days later, they discussed the event, he diplomatically took some of the blame: "I think, Poppy," he said, "that I should probably have pointed out the difficulties with your plan."

Poppy thought about this for a moment. "Well, maybe, Mr. Smudge," she said. "But maybe I shouldn't assume that *everyone* will *always* be pleased to see a glossy black pug and her best friend."

Chapter Five

POPPY AND THE PELLETS

ONLY A WEEK or two after Poppy the Pug and Mr. Smudge made their ill-fated trip to Wenda's White House, the two friends met again in the little neighbourhood park. Danielle had brought Poppy there so she could run around a bit and play with the children, while she, Danielle, sat on a park bench and chatted with Rachael. Baby Gillian, who was only nine months old, sat in her mom's lap, sucked her pacifier, and waved at the older children as they swung on the swings or climbed on the jungle gym.

Mr. Smudge slunk up to Poppy while she was watching a boy swinging as high as he possibly could on a swing. (The boy's name was Jackson, and he was eight years old and *fearless*!)

"Hello, Poppy," said Mr. Smudge.

"Hello, Mr. Smudge," said Poppy.

"Are you and your human on good terms again?" asked Mr. Smudge. He suspected that Danielle had probably been a little cross with Poppy in the wake of her uninvited visit to the playdate group.

"Oh, yes, I've forgiven her," said Poppy, whose memory was perhaps a little faulty when it came to this kind of thing.

"Um, good," said Mr. Smudge. "Have you done anything exciting recently?'

"Not really," said Poppy the Pug. "Except that I've had some wonderful walks. And some wonderful meals. And some very nice cuddles."

"Those all sound like good things," said Mr. Smudge.

"They are," said Poppy. "I'm very kind to my human."

"Do you think you might be able to stay outside and chat when your human goes home?" asked Mr. Smudge.

"Well, we'll see," said Poppy airily. "Sometimes I like to have a drink and a little snack as soon as a walk is over, but maybe after that."

"I'll just be hanging around," said Mr. Smudge. "Give a yip if you do come out again."

"I shall," said Poppy, and Mr. Smudge went off on the cat-trail again, while Poppy resumed watching the children on the swings and jungle gyms, and occasionally offering advice and encouragement in the form of melodic snuffles, barks and sneezes.

★★★

As it happens, Danielle was in a good mood when she got home, and she seemed largely to have forgotten that Poppy had wandered off down the street a week or two before. So after she had given the glossy black pug a snack (and some fresh water), she allowed Poppy to slip outside again, though she did wag an admonishing finger at her. "No straying, Poppy!" she said.

"As if!" Poppy thought indignantly. "Let the world come to me!" And so Poppy went outside, and Danielle left the front door open and the screen on the screen-door up so she could hear Poppy if she barked. And after sniffing the air for a moment or two, and having a bit of a scratch, Poppy gave a yip to let Mr. Smudge know that she was available.

But Mr. Smudge was apparently occupied elsewhere, for he didn't come immediately, and after Poppy had yipped again, and had another scratch, she found she was a little bored. And just as she realized this, she noticed that Wenda's husband at the White House down the street had emerged from the garage, bringing with him a bucket and a wheeled contraption of some kind. She watched with interest.

Wenda's husband fussed with his wheeled contraption for a couple of minutes, and just as he seemed satisfied that it was behaving in the way he wanted it to behave, his wife opened the front door. "Dave!" she screeched. "I need some help!" Dave immediately abandoned what he was doing and moved obediently toward the front door and into the house.

Now, Poppy was a social dog, and she was also very curious about the goings-on in the Thompson Bay neighbourhood. It was, after all, *her* neighbourhood, and this was *her* street, and she felt strongly that she had a responsibility to keep an eye on things. Pugs, she believed, had a very special role to play in making sure that the universe unfolded in the way it should. This belief had been given a boost just the day before when Andrew told her, very solemnly, that in China – a country filled with clever people – pugs had once been known as *sacred lions*.

And so what choice did a sacred lion have but to trot down the street to find out exactly what Dave's wheeled contraption was, and what it might be used for, and what might be in the bucket? When Poppy arrived on Wenda's front lawn she looked around carefully, then sniffed the wheeled thingie, then sniffed the white pellets in the bucket . . . and here's where things became interesting. The white pellets didn't smell like anything Poppy had ever smelled before, so she took another deep sniff – and when that sniff didn't give her any more information, she thought it might be best if she took a mouthful of them just to make sure that they were acceptable in the neighbourhood.

Truth to tell, the white pellets didn't taste very good at all – they were bitter and oily – but Poppy was a fair-minded pug, and she felt it was important to give them a chance, just in case they tasted bad only at first and then began to taste good. She kept munching, then, and eventually swallowed the first mouthful, though she decided almost immediately that she needn't give the white pellets a second chance: they tasted just as horrible after they'd been chewed as they did when she first took them in her mouth.

That said, she felt she'd done the right thing in checking them out . . . and she trotted back home.

Five or six minutes later Poppy began to wonder whether she might in fact have made a mistake. Her little tummy began to feel very upset indeed, and just a few minutes later she began to throw up. And after she threw up once, she threw up again – and then again and again and again . . . and it was at this moment that Mr. Smudge arrived.

"Poppy!" said Mr. Smudge, in some alarm. "What's wrong?"

"My tummy is a little unsettled," said Poppy the Pug, doing her best to sound at once lady-like and lionish. "But I think, Mr. Smudge," she added, "that I need to go to sleep now. I'm very tired. Good night."

Mr. Smudge immediately saw that Poppy was not well at all, so he went to Danielle's screen door and began howling in the way that only an agitated Maine Coon cat can. Fortunately Danielle was not sleeping, and fortunately the screen on the screen door was open, so it only took a moment for Poppy's human companion to come to the door. "What on the earth is the matter?" she asked – but then she saw Poppy lying on the ground with her eyes closed. "Poppy!" she cried.

Poppy's eyes fluttered open for just a moment, but she discovered that even giving a little bark was beyond her, so she closed them again. She really didn't feel well at all, and she felt so very tired, and Mr. Smudge and Danielle seemed very, very far away.

★★★

So it came to pass that Poppy was very sick, and she nearly didn't wake up at all from the sleep she took that afternoon. While she was sleeping, Danielle bundled her up in a blanket and put her in the car and drove very quickly to the pet hospital which was, fortunately, just a couple of miles up the highway. Mr. Smudge tried to get into the car, too, but Danielle didn't understand that he wanted to help and shooed him away.

At the hospital Poppy was looked after by a very nice and very clever man called Dr. Sparling who quickly realized that the little pug must have eaten something poisonous. He gave her a shot of something helpful, and then put her in a special place to keep her warm, and he told Danielle that he and his nurses would keep checking on Poppy through the night and that she, Danielle, should go back home and get some sleep. And after Danielle had had a good cry, during which Dr. Sparling held her hand and gave her lots of tissues, she did as he advised.

Mr. Smudge, meanwhile, was in a terrible state. He was a clever and observant cat, and he had quickly figured out that Poppy had eaten something she shouldn't have – and he couldn't help but wonder if he might have prevented her from doing so if he had arrived at her house just a few moments earlier. This wasn't a very useful thought, because, of course, Poppy's mistake was not Mr. Smudge's fault at all, but animals, like humans, sometimes blame themselves for things they haven't done. So Mr. Smudge sat on Danielle's front door-step and ruminated and swished his tail and felt worse and worse and worse.

Eventually, however, he realized that he should go back to *his* own home, and he set off slowly down the street – and as he was approaching Wenda's White House he saw the wheeled contraption, and the bucket, and he realized, in a great flash of cat-insight that *here* was the cause of Poppy's sickness: a bucket of unguarded, uncovered, *poisonous* white pellets.

In that instant, Mr. Smudge was almost overwhelmed by a rush of sadness and anger: how *could* humans be so careless, he wondered? And, thinking that, he remembered the brave way that Poppy had charged Psycho-Cat just a few short weeks before, and how she had rescued him from the garage, and with these thoughts clearly in his mind he charged the bucket, knocking it over and spilling the white pellets all over the ground. And just as he did this, it began to rain, and as it rained the pellets began to dissolve and run into the ground . . . and though Mr. Smudge couldn't know this, it meant that there was going to be a large patch of dead grass on Wenda's beautifully manicured front lawn.

Three weeks later, when Poppy had mostly recovered, she found herself once again at the little neighbourhood park with Danielle. Danielle sat on the bench, as before, and Poppy sat in her lap, and the two of them watched the children. They had only been there a few minutes when eight-year old Jackson appeared with another little boy. They climbed on the jungle gym, and swung on the swings, and then Jackson saw something colourful in the grass and went over to examine it.

"What is it?" asked the other boy.

"A really big wad of gum," said Jackson.

"I double-dog-dare you to chew on it," said his friend.

"Okay," said Jackson — but before he could do so Poppy was on her feet in Danielle's lap, barking and barking and barking.

"Don't you dare put that in your mouth," Danielle called to Jackson.

"Says who?" said Jackson — who could sometimes be a rather rude little boy.

"Says my dog," said Danielle, hugging Poppy but otherwise keeping her eyes fixed on Jackson. Jackson shrugged and carried the wad of gum to the garbage container a few steps away.

So, yes, Poppy recovered from her sickness, though it was a full month before she felt fully herself again. But Wenda's lawn would take much longer to heal, and Wenda remained cross with her husband, and with the world, for a long, long time.

Chapter Six

POPPY AND THE BAD BOYS

IN THE MIDDLE of the summer, Poppy and Danielle would usually have their long walks in the morning before it got too hot. Danielle didn't teach in July or August, and this meant that she was home pretty well every day. Poppy liked that.

Danielle's man-friend Andrew had to continue working through most of the summer, but he would often take Fridays off and come and spend a long weekend. Poppy enjoyed his visits because Andrew would always bring a meaty treat or two with him, and because he didn't mind now when she curled up on the sofa between him and Danielle when they watched a movie in the evening. Mind you, she wasn't pleased when he shook her awake and complained she was snoring so loud he couldn't hear the television!

"I don't snore," she explained to her friend Mr. Smudge, the Maine Coon cat. "I just breathe *resonantly*. It's part of being a sacred lion."

Of course Mr. Smudge agreed with Poppy that breathing resonantly is a *very* different thing from snoring, and that Andrew really should be able to tell the difference. "Perhaps he's never known a pug before," he suggested.

"Well, that may be true," agreed Poppy. "Pugs are very rare, you know. And our ways are not the ways of ordinary dogs."

"I'm sure that's true," said Mr. Smudge – who was a very diplomatic cat.

The two friends were once again at the playground when they had this conversation.

Danielle didn't take Poppy to the dog park very often these days, because she found that the mothers at the human park didn't seem to mind having Poppy around – so long as she, Danielle, brought her little plastic bags with her. Rachael's Baby Gillian was particularly fond of seeing Poppy. "Dog!" she would say whenever she saw her. "Dog-dog-dog-dog-dog!"

"Humans take a long time to learn language," Poppy explained to Mr. Smudge. "Pugs know *everything* about expressing themselves when they are just a few months old, but humans . . ." She gave an eloquent toss of her head. "Well, they're very slow."

"Ah," said Mr. Smudge gravely. "Poor things," he added, as Poppy seemed to expect a little more from him.

"What's your dog's name?" asked eight-year-old Jackson. He had just appeared at the park – this time with a different boy from the one who had been with him on the day he nearly ate the wad of abandoned gum.

"This is Poppy," said Danielle.

"*Poopy*!" said Jackson. "Hey, Bobby, the dog's name is *Poopy*!" The two boys laughed and laughed — and then forgot all about Poppy as they ran off to join two other boys who were playing with a ball at the basketball court.

"Boys," said Rachael to Danielle. "They really are ridiculous creatures." But she smiled as she said it.

Danielle gave Poppy's head an affectionate ruffle. "Poppy doesn't mind," she said. "She *knows* she's wonderful."

But, truth to tell, Poppy was a little miffed. Poppy was a noble name, after all, while *Poopy* was — well, it just wasn't nice. Poppy gave her ear a good scratch to cheer herself up, and Mr. Smudge pretended that he hadn't heard what Jackson had said. "Dog-dog-dog-dog-dog!" gurgled Baby Gillian.

★★★

Later that day, while Danielle was working in her office, and Mr. Smudge was out on the cat-trail, Poppy was sitting under the shade of a tree on her front lawn when she saw Psycho-Cat come slinking down the other side of the street. She was immediately on her guard, for she knew that Psycho-Cat would not have forgiven her for protecting Mr. Smudge back in the spring. She didn't think that the mean old cat would dare to come into her own yard – not with Danielle just a bark away – but you could never be absolutely sure with Psycho-Cat.

A moment later Psycho-Cat saw her, and he paused. He seemed to be considering his options. Poppy's heart beat just a little faster, and the rate increased when Psycho-Cat crossed the street. She scrambled to her feet.

She scrambled to her feet, but she did not run to the front door: this was *her* house, after all, and *her* yard, and she wasn't going to be frightened by Psycho-Cat or anyone else. She stood her ground and stared at Psycho-Cat.

Psycho-Cat stopped as he drew level with her and looked at her meaningfully, but he didn't come into the yard: "Hello, *pet* dog," he said, his voice showing that he thought the word *pet* was a terrible insult.

"My name is Poppy. Poppy the Pug," said Poppy the Pug.

"Where's that scaredy-cat friend of yours?" asked Psycho-Cat. "Shouldn't you be looking after him, wherever he is?"

"You just leave Mr. Smudge alone," said Poppy. "He's a nice, friendly cat. He'd never try to hurt you or anyone else."

Psycho-Cat stared at her for a long moment, then went on his way without saying anything. This surprised Poppy, but after a couple of minutes she laid down again and had a bit of a snooze. A glossy black pug needs her rest.

★★★

A little later that afternoon Mrs. Cairns, the nice old lady who lived up the street, walked by carrying a pink umbrella to protect her from the sun. Poppy got up and stretched when she saw her, and then went up to her to get a head ruffle.

Mrs. Cairns liked small dogs — and Poppy in particular — and she gave the little pug a warm greeting before continuing on her way. Poppy gave herself a good scratch, then went back in search of shade once again. She had to move from her previous spot because it would soon lose its shade, and it took her a moment to find just the right place to plop herself down.

★★★

A few moments later Mr. Smudge came along the street. He made his way straight to Poppy and laid down beside her. "It's a hot day," he said.

"How are things on the cat-trail?" asked Poppy.

"It's been pretty quiet today," said Mr. Smudge. "I think it's too hot for anyone to do much of anything."

"Psycho-Cat came by a little while ago," said Poppy — and then she yawned. (Pugs are famous for their yawning. They do it at the most surprising times.)

"Did he attack you?" asked Mr. Smudge anxiously.

Poppy thought about telling a little story about how she scared Psycho-Cat away by *roaring* at him, but she decided to stick to the truth. "No," she said. "He just gave me a strange look."

"Good," said Mr. Smudge. "Perhaps he was hot, too."

The two animals chatted about this and that for a while longer, then Mr. Smudge went off in search of his dinner. The walls of his home may have been painted taupe, but Pam was usually good about putting food in his dish at the right times.

★★★

Poppy laid down again. It would soon be time for her dinner too, but it was a lazy sort of day and, unusually for her, she didn't feel *hugely* hungry – or, at least, she felt more tired than hungry. (After all, she had done a lot of socialising that afternoon!) She was just drifting off to sleep again when she saw two boys coming down the street from the same direction that Psycho-Cat had come a little earlier. They were both waving sticks around in the air and talking very loudly.

As Poppy watched the boys come closer to her, Psycho-Cat reappeared at the other end of the street and began moving towards her and the two boys. He was moving quickly, though Poppy noticed that one of his back legs seemed to be hurt. And just a moment later Poppy saw why he was moving at the rate he was: he was being followed by yet another boy, and this boy also had a stick that he was waving around in the air. Poppy stood up.

The two boys saw Psycho-Cat and the single boy at the same time, and the bigger of the two made a kind of whooping noise. They broke out into a run, and the boy behind Psycho-Cat did too, and the result was that the three boys soon had Psycho-Cat penned in between the three of them – and then suddenly they began hitting out at him with their sticks. Psycho-Cat bared his claws and hissed, but he was no match for three boys armed with sticks.

In that instant, Poppy discovered something interesting about herself. She certainly didn't like Psycho-Cat, and she knew in her heart that they could never be friends, but she didn't want to see him hurt either. In fact, Poppy realized – though there wasn't time for her to say this out loud – that she didn't want to see *any* creature hurt. She might sometimes be a rather vain little dog, but she didn't have a mean bone in her glossy black frame, and the thought that Psycho-Cat might be hit hard over and over again made her sad and angry. So she threw back her head and barked and barked and barked!

The front door was flung open and Danielle erupted into the yard, clearly under the impression that her beloved dog was under attack. It took her a moment to realize that wasn't the case, but in that same moment she registered that there were three boys threatening a cat with sticks – and Danielle was as fierce as her pug when it came to defending animals. "You stop that!" she shouted at the boys. "What do you think you're doing? Leave that poor cat alone!"

The three boys froze for a moment, each looking at the others for some sort of leadership or guidance. Finally the biggest boy spoke: "He's just a stupid old Tom-cat," he said.

"I don't care," said Danielle. "You have no right to hurt any animal. How would you feel if someone tried to hurt you? You should be ashamed of yourselves."

The three boys thought about that for a moment, then one by one they lowered their sticks and slunk away, casting backward glances at Danielle but saying nothing.

Poppy looked at Psycho-Cat. Psycho-Cat looked at her, then at Danielle. Then, without a word, he got back on all four paws and headed down the street, taking a different direction from the one the boys had taken.

"Thank goodness you barked," Danielle said to Poppy. "You saved that old Psycho-Cat from being hurt by those bad boys. What a good girl you are, Poppy!"

Poppy thought about that for a moment – then decided that Danielle was right. She also decided that it was time for dinner, and she followed her human companion into the house.

. . . And of course, we don't *know* what the boys thought – but we can hope that they *did* think, and that they decided they would no longer go looking for animals (or people) to hurt. To make that more likely to happen, Danielle did some checking around and telephoned their parents that very evening.

Chapter Seven

POPPY AND MRS. CAIRNS

MRS. CAIRNS WAS a dear old lady who lived just down the street from Danielle and Poppy the Pug. She was seventy-nine years old, she had two grown-up daughters with grown-up children of their own, and she spent her days reading, knitting, writing letters and going for walks. Her husband had died four years previously, and sometimes she missed him terribly – but she took a lot of pleasure from her extended family (for whom she was always knitting sweaters and mittens and toques), and from her books and from her daily walks to the mailbox and the convenience store. Mrs. Cairns liked animals, too, and her walks always took longer than they might have because she stopped to talk to dogs and cats and even the odd squirrel.

One morning in the late summer, a couple of weeks after the Back to School sales had started and teachers were beginning to have nightmares, Mrs. Cairns set out on her usual trip to the mailbox, stopping enroute to talk to Danielle and Poppy (who were on their way to the park). "Hello, Danielle," she said. "And hello to you, too, you dear little dog."

Poppy quite liked being called a *dear little dog*, and she graciously allowed Mrs. Cairns to bend down and ruffle her head.

"Poppy's decided that she's a sacred lion," said Danielle. "Andrew told her that's how pugs are seen in China."

"Well, I'm not surprised," said Mrs. Cairns. "There is something majestically feline about her hind-quarters – though not perhaps her dear little face."

"Poppy thinks she has the *heart* of a lion," said Danielle. "Don't you, Poppy?"

"Well, of course I do," barked Poppy indignantly. "Because I have."

"What a dear little snuffly bark she has," said Mrs. Cairns. "I just wish we knew what she was saying." She gave Poppy's head another ruffle, chatted for just a moment longer with Danielle, then went on her way to the mailbox, leaving a strong scent of lavender behind her. Danielle and Poppy proceeded to the park.

The park was quite crowded on this day. It was as though much of the Thompson Bay neighbourhood had woken up that morning, realized how close it was to the beginning of September, and resolved to make the most of what time remained. There were at least seven mothers with children there, but there were also four dads, and two grandmothers, and one grandfather, and a fair number of children old enough not to need their parents there with them. Danielle talked with a couple of her neighbours for a moment or two, then joined Rachael and little Baby Gillian on the bench they usually shared. "Dog-dog-dog-dog-dog!" said Baby Gillian, who was, as always, delighted to see Poppy.

While Danielle and Rachael chatted about their favourite female authors, Poppy watched the children playing on the swings and the jungle gyms. It warmed her heart to see them, and it reminded her of her own puppy days which were not, after all, that far behind her. And it warmed her heart even more when she saw her friend Mr. Smudge the Maine Coon cat making his way through the groups of children to join her.

"It's a funny thing, Danielle, but I think that big cat and Poppy are friends," said Rachael.

"I think you're right," said Danielle. "He often comes over when I let Poppy go outside. He lies beside her on the lawn, and it's almost as if they were having a conversation."

"I think that's sweet," said Rachael.

"Dog-dog-dog-dog—*cat*!" said Baby Gillian. (Or, at least, what she said sounded a *little* like cat.)

A few minutes later a swarm of boys arrived, the *fearless* Jackson among them. They didn't bother the smaller children, however, instead heading straight to the outdoor basketball court where they began to play a spirited game of dodge-ball. "At least they're not beating each other up," said Rachael to Danielle.

"I don't quite know what to make of boys," said Danielle.

"I've known some very nice ones," said Rachael, "but I don't think they know what to do with themselves sometimes."

"I know some nice ones, too," said Danielle, "but they do take a long time to grow up."

"They're a little like wine, then, aren't they?" said Rachael. "They need time to mature."

"Speaking of wine," said Danielle, "why don't you come over for a glass this evening? Do you think your husband would look after baby Gillian?"

"Oh, I know he would," said Rachael. "And yes, I'd like that."

★★★

After Danielle and Poppy had eaten their suppers – and Poppy's was the best she had ever tasted! – Danielle did some cleaning up around the house. She washed the dishes, mopped the bathroom floor, and vacuumed the living room. "This is one of the reasons I have guests," she told Poppy, "because it forces me to do some house-cleaning."

As always, Poppy watched the process disapprovingly. Anything that destroyed the natural disorder of the household troubled her: she felt that a home should ideally have little piles of interesting things all over the place – little piles that a sacred lion could romp in and sleep on, if she felt so inclined. She found the vacuuming the worst insult of all: not only was it far too noisy, but it almost erased the evidence that she occupied the space. She retreated to her bedroom – the one she let Danielle share – until the whole business was over.

An hour or so later there came a knock at the door and Danielle welcomed Rachael into their home for the first time. Rachael had brought a plate of cookies with her, and she earned Poppy's good will by giving her one of them. "I made that one without sugar," she told Danielle.

"That was very thoughtful of you," said Danielle – and Poppy agreed. She felt immediately that Danielle should invite Rachael over more often.

"Well," said Danielle, "you don't have your baby with you, so I'm going to put my own little fur-baby outside for a while."

Normally Poppy would have been offended at being put outside, but she was very rarely let out at dusk and she welcomed the chance to see the night settle on the neighbourhood. She also suspected that Mr. Smudge might be out on one of his night prowls, and she thought it might be nice to lie on the lawn and talk about things. She wanted to tell him about her dinner, and about the cookie that Rachael had given her, and ask whether his human companion Pam was as silly about vacuuming as Danielle was.

There was still a little light left when Danielle opened the front door, and Poppy stepped out and looked around with interest. Even more interesting than the sights, of course, were the smells: she knew just by sniffing the air what people had had for their dinners in every house on the street, and the scent of barbecue on a late summer's evening was particularly pleasing to a meat-eating pug. Poppy loved Danielle with all her puggy heart and soul, but she rather wished she were the sort of companion who had a barbecue. She was very fond of Andrew, too, but he hadn't bought Danielle a barbecue, and Poppy thought that was surely the first gift a good boyfriend should buy his girl.

Poppy gave a little yip in the hope that Mr. Smudge might hear, and a moment or two later she heard a distant meow – coming, she guessed, from about two blocks away. She knew it would take her feline friend a couple of minutes to make the trip, so she settled down on the front lawn with a contented sigh to wait for him.

But even as Poppy settled her tummy down on the grass, she smelled something that wasn't food. It was a woodsy smell – but not the kind of woodsy smell that a backyard fire pit might give off. It was the smell of wood that had been covered in paint, and there was an undernote of burning plastic as well . . . and the smell seemed to be coming from Mrs. Cairns' house just down the street. Poppy stood up again.

At just that same moment Mr. Smudge appeared, rounding the corner at the opposite end of the street from Wenda's White House, and his route took him right by Mrs. Cairns' home. Poppy trotted towards him – partly because she was glad to see him, but also because she wanted to see what might be producing the vaguely disturbing odours from the house.

Glossy black pug and Maine Coon cat met right in front of Mrs. Cairns' house. "Mr. Smudge," said Poppy, "do you smell what I'm smelling?"

Mr. Smudge stopped and sniffed the air, turning towards the small bungalow as he did so. "It's smoke," he said. "Smoke and wood and paint – and maybe a little plastic as well. And carpet," he added, as the scents became thicker and more complex.

The two animals stood and stared at the house, and suddenly Poppy saw a little flicker of yellow through one of the windows and she knew – she *knew* – that something was wrong. "Fire!" she said. "There's a *fire!*" And "fire!" she barked. "*Fire! Fire! FIRE!*" She ran back towards her own home, barking wildly, and Mr. Smudge followed, hard on her heels.

Danielle came out of her front door just as Poppy arrived, all out of breath, at the front step. "What on earth is wrong, Poppy?" she asked.

"Fire!" barked Poppy. "Fire at Mrs. Cairns' house! Call someone! Do something!"

Rachael appeared a moment later, looking over Danielle's shoulder. "What's upsetting her?" she asked. And then: "Oh. Where's that smoky smell coming from?"

"Mrs. Cairns' house!" barked Poppy. "There's a *fire*!" And to underline the news she ran back to the road and barked at Mrs. Cairns' place, then returned to Danielle and Rachael at the front step. "*Fire! Fire! FIRE!*"

"Do you think there could be a fire at Mrs. Cairns' home?" said Danielle to Rachael.

"Is that her house down the street?" asked Rachael. "The one with the front door painted blue? Oh, is that a wisp of smoke coming out the window on the side?"

"Yes! Yes!" barked Poppy. "That's what I'm trying to tell you! There's a fire there! *Do something*!"

The two women stood and stared down the street for a moment, then Danielle made a decision. "I think Poppy's trying to tell us that there's a fire there. I'm calling the fire department." She went back into the house and grabbed her cell phone, then returned to the front door.

"I think we should go down to the house and bang on the door," said Rachael.

"Good idea," said Danielle, who was already dialling 911. The two women set off at a half-run down the road, with Poppy and Mr. Smudge right behind them. When they all arrived, Danielle and Rachael ran right up to Mrs. Cairns' front door and banged on it. Because there wasn't an immediate answer, they tried the handle – but the door was locked. There was no question, however, that there was a sort of crackling sound coming from inside.

Poppy stood on the front lawn with one of her front paws raised, sniffing the air and listening as carefully as she knew how. She *sensed* that her friend Mrs. Cairns wasn't in the front part of the house, and so, after a moment or so, she raced around to the back yard, Mr. Smudge right behind her.

"Poppy! *Poppy*!" cried Danielle, worried that the little pug was going to put herself in harm's way.

"Let's see where she's going!" said Rachael, and so the two women followed the little dog and the big cat round the house to find Poppy scuffling frantically at the sliding door to the walk-out basement. With the wail of fire sirens sounding in the distance but getting rapidly nearer, Rachael and Danielle joined Poppy at the sliding door and pressed their faces against the glass: after their eyes had adjusted to the darkness inside, they could see a crumpled figure on the floor – its outline made clearer by a growing yellow glow from the top of the basement stairs.

"Oh dear, oh dear, oh dear!" said Danielle – or, at least, she said *something* like that. She quickly discovered that the sliding glass door was also locked, and she and Rachael began looking around for something to break the thick glass. Poppy, meanwhile, had raced back around the house to greet the fire-engine, which had just screeched to a stop in front of the bungalow.

"Follow me! Follow me! Follow me!" barked Poppy as the firemen jumped off the truck and began heading toward the front door. Remarkably, though, one of the firemen *did* follow her, his fire-fighting experience having taught him to trust dogs – and just a few seconds later he rounded the house and joined Rachael and Danielle in the back yard.

"The door's locked and we can see Mrs. Cairns lying on the ground!" said Danielle.

"Right," said the fireman, who just happened to be Jackson's dad! He took an axe from his belt. "Stand back!" he said, and he swung the axe right through the glass, then put his hand through the hole and unlocked the screen door. A moment later he was inside – at just about the same instant that his fellow fire-fighters broke through the front door. And in just a few moments they had Mrs. Cairns safely out of the house, and the fire, which had started in the kitchen, under control.

★★★

Two days later, on a Saturday afternoon, Danielle and Andrew were sitting in Danielle's living room having a cup of tea. Danielle was telling Andrew about what had happened on the night of the fire, and Andrew was making impressed noises at all the right moments.

"You know, Dani," said Andrew – *Dani* was his nickname for Danielle – "I used to be annoyed by dogs barking, but in the last little while Poppy the Pug's barking has saved an old Tom cat *and* a dear old lady." He stroked the head of the little pug, who was lying in his lap.

"Well, of course," said Danielle. "Poppy is a very clever dog. She has a special bark that she uses just for emergencies."

Poppy raised her head suddenly: she had just heard something unusual and unexpected.

"What is it, Poppy?" asked Andrew as the little pug headed for the front door.

Danielle opened the door and there, to everyone's surprise, was a big red fire-truck on the road. Advancing up the driveway towards them was Jackson's father, Rick the Fireman, carrying a tiny firefighter's hat.

"Hello, guys," he said cheerfully. "I've got a little present for your pug. It's a thank you for her outstanding service to community safety."

"Oh, Poppy, look!" said Danielle, taking the gift from Rick. She placed the hat, which had a Velcro strap, on Poppy's head.

Poppy wasn't altogether sure she liked the feel of the hat. But she recognized that the human meant well, so she put up with wearing it while Rick, Danielle, Andrew and some of the neighbours took pictures of her with their cell-phones.

But it's perhaps a good thing that pugs can't read, because Rick, who had relied on his son Jackson for information, had had a slightly inaccurate name printed on the front of the helmet. "*Poopy* the Pug," it said.

Chapter Eight

Poppy and the Little Girl

One beautiful Saturday afternoon in late September, Poppy took Andrew for a walk around the neighbourhood. (That, in any event, was how *she* saw it – because, after all, she had to lead *him*.) Andrew enjoyed his walks with Poppy: he was, of course, fond of the little dog herself, but he also enjoyed the attention he got from people in the neighbourhood when he walked her. "The only better way of meeting women would be if I had a baby in a Snugli," he teased Danielle before they left the house.

Danielle rolled her eyes at him. "Poppy's the only baby I need," she said. "And you behave yourself."

Poppy and Andrew walked along Danielle's street (Bissonnette), and then took Scollard Drive all the way to the top of the hill – and then down the other side to the neighbourhood park. "Why doesn't Scollard Drive have sidewalks?" Andrew asked Poppy, a little irritated that they had to walk in the road.

Poppy didn't answer. She was intent on getting to the park, and hoping, of course, that she might see her friend Mr. Smudge there.

Once at the park, Andrew and Poppy walked around the perimeter so that Poppy could sniff the bushes and long grasses, and then made their way to the swings and jungle gyms and slide, where they sat down to watch the children. Andrew didn't know many people there because he lived somewhere else during the week, so he didn't recognize Wenda from the White House when she approached him.

"I hope you're keeping that dog on a leash," Wenda said.

"Yes, I am, actually," said Andrew, raising the leash from his lap slightly.

"She snuck into my house one day and *terrified* all the babies and moms who were visiting," said Wenda — and in saying this she was not being truthful. (It's a sad thing, but adults don't always tell the truth any more than children do.)

"Ah," said Andrew, suddenly realizing who Wenda was. (Danielle had, of course, told him about Poppy's ill-advised visit to Wenda's house.) "Well," he said, "rest assured that I have this Big Fierce Dog well under control."

Wenda stared at him suspiciously, but Andrew looked so serious that she couldn't really complain any more. "Good," she said — and she stalked off to tell another mother that her child was making too much noise. Poppy sneezed after her.

Andrew found that his enjoyment of the park had been spoiled by his conversation with

Wenda, so it wasn't long before he rose and gave the tiniest of tugs on the leash. "Up you get, Poppy," he said. "We'll head home and see if Danielle can take a break from her marking." Mr. Smudge had not come by, so Poppy got up willingly enough and the two of them headed home along Cunningham Boulevard.

On the way along Cunningham, Andrew and Poppy came across Mrs. Cairns and one of her grown-up daughters. Mrs. Cairns had survived the fire at her home, but she had not yet moved back into the house (which was undergoing some repairs). Her daughters, however, took turns bringing her back to the neighbourhood for her usual walks.

"There's that dear little dog who saved my life," said Mrs. Cairns – and she introduced her daughter to Poppy and Andrew. "I was going down the stairs to call the fire brigade," she said, "and I tripped – and if it hadn't been for dear little Poppy I wouldn't be alive today."

"Poppy's pretty special," said Andrew, and he waited in a friendly way while Mrs. Cairns and her daughter Brigid made a fuss over the glossy black pug.

★★★

Later that day, after Poppy had had her dinner, and while Andrew and Danielle were lingering over theirs, there came a frantic knock at the front door. Poppy immediately woke from a peaceful nap and ran to the door barking – just in case Danielle and Andrew had not heard. There, on the doorstep, was a young teenage girl, and she looked very upset.

"Have you seen a little three-year-old girl?" she asked. "Her name's Min."

"No," said Danielle, who had opened the door. "How long has she been missing?"

"I don't know," said the girl, and she suddenly burst into tears. "I'm the babysitter," she sobbed, "and I was looking after her, and a friend called me on my cell, and she was really sad. So I was talking to her, and suddenly I looked up and Min was gone!"

"We'll come and help you look," said Danielle. She and Andrew grabbed their keys and headed out the door, and Poppy slipped out with them. Meanwhile, the teenage girl went and knocked on the front door of Danielle's next door neighbours, AJ and Ian.

"Have you called the police?" Andrew called across the driveway to the teenage girl. It had suddenly occurred to him that the police would be very helpful.

"Ian *is* a policeman," said Danielle, referring to her next door neighbour. "Do you want to check back yards on this street, Andrew? I'll go to the next."

"Right," said Andrew. He quickly ran into Danielle's back yard, intending to move from yard to yard all the way down Bissonnette, checking behind bushes and tool sheds in the process.

"Come with me, Poppy!" said Danielle, noticing that her pug was with her. "We'll go and search on McAuliffe Street!"

Poppy followed Danielle, and stayed with her while she knocked at two front doors on

McAuliffe. But when Danielle went with the second home-owner into her back yard to check a little playhouse, Poppy saw Mr. Smudge across the street and ran over to greet him. "Mr. Smudge, Mr. Smudge," she yipped. "We're looking for a little girl called Min who slipped away from her babysitter!"

"That's not good," said Mr. Smudge worriedly. "It will be completely dark soon. What are your human companions doing?"

"They're checking back yards," said Poppy. "Danielle has just gone behind this house."

"Well, that's probably a good idea," said Mr. Smudge. "But do you think a little girl would go into a strange back yard?"

"I don't know," said Poppy. "Perhaps we should do our best to *think* like a little girl and see what happens."

She sat down on her hind legs and thought hard, and to assist the process gave her right ear a good scratch. In the meantime, she saw, several people had come out of their homes to join the search.

"What places in the neighbourhood do little girls and little boys like to visit?" asked Mr. Smudge.

"The park!" said Poppy excitedly. "They like the park!"

"That's true," said Mr. Smudge. "But for that reason I imagine that the humans will check there. In fact," he added, "I bet there are some humans there still, and will be until it's completely dark."

Poppy knew he was right. The park was a popular place at this time of year. Moms and dads would take their children there after dinner, and just as *they* were leaving a group of teenagers often arrived and sat talking and texting on the benches overlooking the jungle gym. "If I were a little girl," Poppy said slowly, "I would want to go and play at the . . ." She thought hard. "I would want to go and play at the . . ."

Mr. Smudge looked at her expectantly.

"I would want to go and play at the . . . pond!" Poppy looked at Mr. Smudge. "She could be at the pond!"

Now the pond wasn't really a pond. It was a place in the neighbourhood that had been excavated (which means *dug out*) to form a drainage area. It was where the rainwater ran when it rained very heavily, and there were reeds and bulrushes in it, and trees had been planted around it. It looked like a natural spot even though humans had designed and engineered it. And, yes, it was just the kind of place that a little girl or boy might go, if only because their parents had told them *not* to go there unless they were with a trusted grown-up. And it was also the kind of place where a child might fall in if she wasn't very, very careful.

Poppy and Mr. Smudge raced off to the pond as fast as their little legs would take them, passing a man and woman about the same age as Danielle and Andrew who were carrying flashlights and calling, "Min! Min!"

By the time the two animals arrived at the pond it was already dusk, and the frogs had begun their evening chorus. The large cat and the small dog paused on the slope leading down to the water and looked around carefully. At first they saw nothing, but then, emerging from behind a stand of reeds, they saw a tiny figure in a shirt with a hoodie, a skirt and dark leggings. This figure seemed to be following something – perhaps a moth – though the growing darkness made it hard to see. And just an instant after they saw her – for it was a little girl – she tripped and fell. They heard a splash, and the two friends knew in an instant that she had fallen face first into the water.

Sometimes there isn't time to think. Poppy and Mr. Smudge shot towards the little girl, racing around the pond with such speed and determination that the frogs were shocked into silence. Mr. Smudge arrived first, and he stood helpless by the side of the pond staring into the water. The back of the small figure was just barely above the surface, and the little girl was struggling, but she couldn't raise her head out of the water.

Poppy arrived an instant later. She too stood on the side of the pond and barked once – but she immediately saw that the little girl was unable to rescue herself, no matter what advice Poppy offered. The little dog jumped up and down once, twice, then threw herself into the water. She grabbed the small human by her hoodie and, using all her strength, dragged her to the bank.

"She's not moving!" said Mr. Smudge. And it was true: the little girl – Min – had sucked a lot of water into her lungs, and she was at risk of drowning even though she was now out of the pond.

"I don't know what else to do!" said Poppy, panting. It seemed so unfair. She had pulled the little girl from the water – couldn't she at least breathe on her own? Mr. Smudge went up to the small figure and nuzzled up under her arm, as if he were hoping to revive her with his body warmth.

And then something remarkable happened – something completely strange and unexpected and astounding. *Psycho-Cat* suddenly appeared out of the gathering dark. For just a fraction of a second Poppy wondered if he was going to attack her or Mr. Smudge, but Psycho-Cat wasn't looking at them at all.

The big, bad-tempered Tom-cat crouched, launched himself into the air, then came down on Min's little chest with all four of his paws. A big cat can weigh around twenty pounds, and twenty pounds dropped on a small human's chest carries a great deal of force. When Psycho-Cat landed, the contact he made forced at least some of the water from Min's lungs, and she began to cough and sputter. At just that moment, fortunately, a couple of grown-up humans arrived, and to Poppy and Mr. Smudge's great relief they knew exactly what to do.

And what of Psycho-Cat? He disappeared into the night as quietly and mysteriously as he had come.

★★★

Later that night, after little Min had been checked out by a paramedic *and* by a doctor, and her parents had arrived back from the movies, and the teenage babysitter had promised everyone in sight that she would never lose herself in her cell-phone again, Danielle and Andrew sat in the living room talking about the day. Poppy had been given a bath to get the pond mud off her, and a bone as a reward for her hard work. She was feeling warm and cozy and appreciated – though she didn't think Danielle had really needed to use soap during the bath.

"This is one remarkable pug," said Andrew, putting down his mug of tea with one hand and ruffling Poppy's head with the other.

"She is," said Danielle fondly. "She's my own precious, life-saving fur-baby."

"You know," said Andrew, "when I first met her I thought she was a bit spoiled . . . but she's certainly showed she can do remarkable things."

"Of course I can," thought Poppy. "I'm a sacred lion." But she didn't say anything out loud. It had been a good evening, and she was looking forward to talking with Mr. Smudge about their adventure tomorrow – or perhaps the day after that. And she was confident – as confident as a glossy black pug could be – that she and Mr. Smudge had many more exciting adventures ahead of them.

Acknowledgements

I am grateful to a number of good folk who have read the manuscript of *A Pug Called Poppy* and offered helpful commentary. Let me mention in particular:

Muriel, Rachael and Nina Mason
Denise Adele Heaps
Rachael Stapleton
Brenda Baker
Greg, Keaton and Mikayla Girard
Jessica and Gillian Knoyle
Terry, Aria and Noa Ross
Andrew Sparling